MY FRIEND JAMAL

STORY AND
PHOTOGRAPHY BY
**ANNA
MCQUINN**

ARTWORK BY
BEN FREY

annick press
toronto + new york + vancouver

My friend is Somali—but he was born here—in Queen Charlotte's Hospital, just down the road. Same as me!
2
3
4
9
10
11
18

We were born in the exact same month, so we started kindergarten at the same time. We've been friends ever since.

My name is Joseph. His name is Jamal.

When Jamal started kindergarten, he could only say a few English words, but we were still best friends.

Now we talk all the time—except when Miss Hall makes us sit apart—for talking too much!

Sometimes Jamal comes to my house.

His mom told my mom that he's not allowed to eat sausages, because he's a Muslim and he doesn't eat pork. He can't drink milk either, because he has eczema.

Sometimes I go to Jamal's house.

It smells different from ours because his mom cooks with special spices.

At Jamal's we get to eat sitting on the floor. It's like a picnic every day!

My favorite thing to eat at Jamal's house is Sabayad, which is a kind of pancake.

When we have pasta, Jamal's mom puts a banana in it—which sounds weird but tastes awesome.

I asked my mom if we could have banana in our pasta at home. She says she'll think about it.

When we are at Jamal's house, mostly we play at being superheroes. Jamal has a neat outfit he got for his birthday. Usually he wears the suit and I wear the cape...

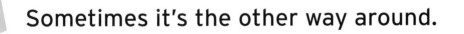

Sometimes it's the other way around.

At my house, we play basketball. I can do crossovers and Jamal can bounce behind his back! He has a real jersey he got from his cousin.

When we're big, we're going to play on the same team and live in a huge house and have a monster car like the ones on TV. I want it to be an SUV and Jamal wants a Hummer—we argue about it all the time.

Sometimes when I'm at Jamal's house, his mom goes in her bedroom and prays. She prays at one o'clock and six o'clock.

Jamal showed me their Koran—it has a soft velvet cover and looks like our Bible. Inside, it's full of squiggly writing. Jamal says it's Arabic.

He's going to learn to read it when he's older.

Jamal's mom and dad were born in Somalia, in Africa—but a lot of fighting started and people were getting killed. It was very dangerous, so they had to escape.

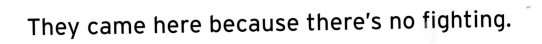

They came here because there's no fighting.

Jamal says sometimes his mom gets very lonely for Somalia. He says she misses the sun and her mom—but she doesn't miss the fighting.

There wasn't always fighting. When she was little, she and her sisters could play outside. She had lots of friends and she rode a bike.

At the end of the year, we had a big concert at school. All our moms and dads came. Jamal and I sang a song together—then we had a party.

All the moms had cooked different things. My mom made spinach and cheese pierogies. It's my Polish grandmother's secret recipe. Jamal ate six!

Everybody got dressed up for the party. Jamal wore a fancy jacket with shiny buttons on it.

I wore the new shirt my dad bought for me.

I met one of Jamal's aunts at the party. She was wearing jeans and a sweatshirt.

I thought if you were Somali you had to wear Somali clothes, but she said you can still be a Somali in jeans!

His aunt didn't wear a headscarf like Jamal's mom. I asked her why not and she said she only wears it when she prays.

I asked her lots of questions.

Jamal's mom knows Somali and Arabic and Italian, which is a lot! But she had to go to college to learn English.

Now she is learning computers. Sometimes Jamal has to help her with her homework. I think it's funny for a kid to help his mom.

My mom helps me with my homework. I'm glad I don't have to help her.

I feel sorry for Jamal because he has never met his grandma—she lives in Somalia and it's too dangerous for him to visit.

My grandma comes to our house every Wednesday and brings me chocolate.

Jamal went to England this summer to visit his cousins. I wasn't sorry for him then. I was jealous—I've never been on an airplane.

But then he brought me a present and I wasn't jealous any more. I was glad he was back because Jamal is my best friend.

I want to say thank you to Milgo and Ayan for answering all my questions, to Jamal for lending us his name, and to Jamilla, Sulaika and Yvonne for their help. I want to thank Anne-Marie and Kevin, Shamsa and Hassan for their hospitality and patience with my constant presence in their homes. Finally, I want to thank two wonderful boys—Liam is my new friend and Mohamed has been an inspiration for a long time.

This book is dedicated to Brian, the little piece of home I brought with me.

© 2008 Anna McQuinn (text and photos)
© 2008 Ben Frey (artwork)
Annick Press Ltd.

All photos by Anna McQuinn and artwork by Ben Frey unless specified otherwise: skyline, pasta, curtains: © Ben Frey; notepaper: © istockphoto.com/Michael Henderson; student at desk, superhero, women and bicycle, sandwiches, pierogies, buns, cake, fruit salad, water bottle, cupcakes,: © istockphoto.com; racing flag: © istockphoto.com/Ryan Burke; BMX rider: © istockphoto.com/Robert Simon; toy car: © istockphoto.com/Krzysztof Krzyscin ; rhinoceros: © istockphoto.com/Liz Leyden; pizza: © istockphoto.com/Vasko Miokovic; sandwich: © istockphoto.com/Kelly Cline; pots: © istockphoto.com/Stuart Pitkin; Hummer: © istockphoto.com/Richard Scherzinger; SUV: © istockphoto.com/ Avesun; Koran: © istockphoto.com/Steven Allan; palm trees (closeup): © istockphoto.com/Pierrette Guertin; rubble pile: © istockphoto.com/Aaron Kohr; photo illustration of Somali soldiers, Mogadishu (1528421): © AP Photo/Karel Prinsloo; kids playing soccer: © istockphoto.com/Donald Gargano; grass: © istockphoto.com/Kutay Tanir; tree: © istockphoto.com/Christine Balderas; chestnut tree: © istockphoto.com/Andrey Prokhorov; girl running, girl walking, palm trees (background), blue flower fabric: © istockphoto.com/Peeter Viisimaa; Fiat: © istockphoto.com/ Loic Bernard; audience (two photos): © istockphoto.com/Don Bayley; samosas: © istockphoto.com/Laurent Renault; juice: © istockphoto.com/Ronald Bloom; cookies: © istockphoto.com/April Martine; donuts: © istockphoto.com/ Saskia Massink; chips: © istockphoto.com/Kati Molin; red balloon: © istockphoto.com/Clayton Hansen; pie: © istockphoto.com/Dawn Liljenquist; African street scene: © istockphoto.com/Raimond Siebesma; polar bear: istockphoto.com/Petr Mašek; cacti: istockphoto.com/Mark Coffey; dolphin: © istockphoto.com/Graham Heywood; toy plane: © istockphoto.com/Daniel Timiraos

Copy edited by Elizabeth McLean
Cover and interior design by Irvin Cheung / iCheung Design, inc.

We acknowledge the support of the Canada Council for the Arts, the Ontario Arts Council, and the Government of Canada through the Book Publishing Industry Development Program (BPIDP) for our publishing activities.

ONTARIO ARTS COUNCIL
CONSEIL DES ARTS DE L'ONTARIO

Cataloguing in Publication
McQuinn, Anna
    My friend Jamal / story and photography by Anna McQuinn ; artwork by Ben Frey.

(My friend—series)
ISBN 978-1-55451-123-5 (bound).—ISBN 978-1-55451-122-8 (pbk.)

    I. Frey, Ben II. Title. III. Title: Jamal. IV. Series.

PZ7.M247My 2008   j823'.92   C2007-905502-8

Printed and bound in China

Published in the U.S.A. by
Annick Press (U.S.) Ltd.

www.annickpress.com

Distributed in Canada by
Firefly Books Ltd.
66 Leek Crescent
Richmond Hill, ON
L4B 1H1

Distributed in the U.S.A. by
Firefly Books (U.S.) Inc.
P.O. Box 1338
Ellicott Station
Buffalo, NY 14205